D0031899

Weekly Reader Children's Book Club presents

HARRY AND SHELLBURT

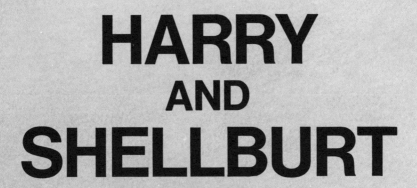

HARRY
AND
SHELLBURT

By Dorothy O. Van Woerkom

Pictures by
Erick Ingraham

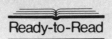

Ready-to-Read

MACMILLAN PUBLISHING CO., INC.
New York
COLLIER MACMILLAN PUBLISHERS
London

Copyright © 1977 Dorothy O. Van Woerkom
Copyright © 1977 Erick Ingraham

All rights reserved. No part of this book may be reproduced
or transmitted in any form or by any means, electronic or
mechanical, including photocopying, recording or by any
information storage and retrieval system, without
permission in writing from the Publisher.

Macmillan Publishing Co., Inc.
866 Third Avenue, New York, N.Y. 10022
Collier Macmillan Canada, Ltd.

Printed in the United States of America

10   9   8   7   6   5   4   3   2   1

LIBRARY OF CONGRESS CATALOGING IN PUBLICATION DATA

Van Woerkom, Dorothy.
  Harry and Shellburt.

  (Ready-to-read)
  SUMMARY: Harry and Shellburt, two good friends,
rerun the classic race between the tortoise and
the hare.
  [1. Friendship—Fiction. 2. Animals—Fiction]
I. Ingraham, Erick. II. Title.
PZ7.V39Har   [E]   77-5352
ISBN 0-02-791290-6

Weekly Reader Children's Book Club Edition

For Joan Lowery Nixon

Harry the Hare
was having dinner
with Shellburt the Tortoise.
"This is a fine
lettuce salad," Harry said.
"What are those
good black things?"

7

"Those are flies,"
Shellburt said.
"I always put flies
in my lettuce salad."

Suddenly
Harry looked sick.
"I am sorry I asked,"
he said.

MONROE LIBRARY

9

Shellburt popped a fly
into his mouth.
"You do not have to
eat the flies," he said.
"Leave them for me."

Harry smiled.
He said, "I like you,
Shellburt. You are easy
to get along with."

"I like you, too,"
said Shellburt.
"But did you know
that once upon a time
hares did not like
tortoises at all?"

"Why was that?"
Harry asked.
He helped himself
to more salad —
but without flies.

"Because," said Shellburt,
"a long time ago
a tortoise won a race
with a hare."

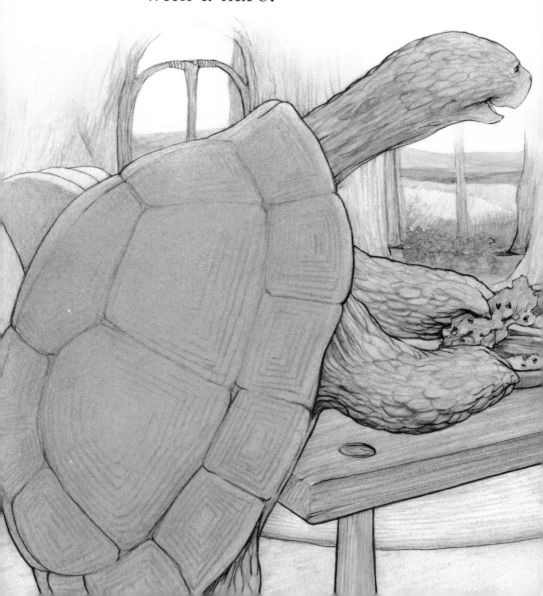

Harry laughed.
"How could a big,
slow tortoise
ever win a race
with a hare?"

Shellburt leaned back
in his chair.
He put his feet up
on a stool.

"Let me tell you
how it was," he said.
And Shellburt told Harry
the tale of the hare
and the tortoise.

"This tortoise wanted
to race," said Shellburt.
"But the hare
just laughed."
"I would laugh, too,"
Harry said.
"Be quiet and listen,"
Shellburt told him.
"The hare and
the tortoise
started out together.
But the hare ran
very fast, and soon
the tortoise was left
far behind."

Harry nodded his head.
But he kept quiet
and listened.
Shellburt said,
"The hare ran
a long way.
He looked back,
but he did not see
the tortoise.
So the hare thought
he would stop
and take a nap."

Harry got up.
He began to jump
up and down.
"That silly hare!"
he shouted.
"What a dumb thing to do!
Was he still asleep
when the tortoise
came by?"

Shellburt ate
another fly.
"Oh, yes," he said.
"And of course
the tortoise
won the race."

"That would never happen
again," Harry said.
"If you and I
had a race,
I would win it."

"Is that so?"
said Shellburt.
"Why don't we just
see about that?"

Harry pointed
out the window.
There was a path
that led to the forest.
"There is a big
wild cabbage
near the forest,"
he said. "Tomorrow
I will race you to it."

27

Early the next morning,
Harry and Shellburt
started off down
the path together.
Harry ran very fast.
Soon Shellburt was left
far behind.

But the sun was hot
and the path was dusty.
Harry stopped near
a pile of rocks.

"I will take a
short nap," he said.
"Only I will wake up
in time! I will not
be like that *other* hare."

Harry found a stick.
It looked like
a big fork.

He put the stick down
on the path.
The long end
pointed the way
to the forest.

"When Shellburt
crawls over this stick
his shell will get caught
in the fork," Harry said.
"He will try to get free,
and I will hear him."

So Harry went to sleep
by the pile of rocks.

Shellburt came by.
He saw the stick.
He saw Harry asleep
by the pile of rocks.
"I know what
that hare is up to,"
he said. "He thinks
my shell will get caught
and I will make a noise."

Shellburt
picked up the stick
and turned it around.
He was careful
not to make a sound!

Then he hurried
on his way.

But now
the long end
of Harry's stick
pointed back
to the starting place.

Harry did not wake up
for a long time.
At last he opened his eyes.
Then he rubbed them.
"What is the matter
with my stick?"
he said.

"It looks all wrong.
I must have
turned around
in my sleep."

He thought for a minute.
"But I am still
ahead of Shellburt,"
he said. "If my stick
had caught him
I would know it!"

And he ran
back up the path
the way he had come.

He thought he was
finishing the race.
"I will try
not to laugh
when Shellburt finds me
waiting for him,"
Harry said.

He ran and ran
and ran.
"This path seems
twice as long
as it ever was,"
Harry said.
"I wonder why?"

At last he stopped.
"Oh, look!" he cried.
"There is
Shellburt's house!
How did I get here?"

Harry knocked
on Shellburt's door.
"Come in!" said Shellburt.
"You are just in time
for lunch."

Harry said,
"I am all mixed up.
I thought I was
racing you
to the big wild
cabbage."

"You were," Shellburt said.
"But you fell asleep.
I turned your stick around
and beat you
to the cabbage.
Then I took
the shortcut home."

Shellburt put a bowl
on the table.
"Here is the cabbage
in this salad," he said.
"I was hoping
you could stay for lunch."

Harry stayed for lunch
with Shellburt.
"This is a fine
cabbage salad," he said.
"Thank you,"
said Shellburt.
"I am glad we had
that race."

"Why?" asked Harry.
"Are you glad because
you won the race?"

"No," Shellburt said.
"I am glad because
I just found out
that flies taste good
with *cabbage,* too!"